SLAM &  W9-AMN-761

Go to the Moon

Written by Chris Sawyer
Illustrated by Dennis Hockerman

Hooked On Phonics

Copyright © 1998 Gateway Learning Corporation. All rights reserved. Printed in China. No part of this publication may be reproduced, stored in any retrieval system or transmitted, in any form or by any means, electronic, mechanical, photocopying, recording, or otherwise, without the prior written permission of the publisher.
ISBN 1-887942-37-8   First Edition   6 7 8 9 10

Slam and Dunk are on the hill.
"What can we do?" asks Dunk.

BUZZ! **THUD!** HISS!

"What is that?" asks Slam.

Slam and Dunk look down
the hill.
"Look! What is that?" says Slam.
"It's a ship!" Dunk says.

"I am Moon Man.
 I am from the moon."
"Hi," say Slam and Dunk.
"My ship is stuck," Moon Man
 says. "I need to fix it."

"We can fix it with you,"
says Slam.

BAM! JAB! WHAM!

CHOP! ZAP!

"It's all set," Moon Man says.
"Can you come with me to
the moon?"
"Yes!" says Slam. "But we need
to check with my mom."

"Mom! Can we go to
the moon?" asks Slam.
"OK, kids. But get back
at six!" says Mom.

Slam and Dunk yell, "Let's go!"
Moon Man steps on the gas.
Up, up, up zips the ship.

Then down, down, down
to the moon.

"Look!" says Slam.
"We can play basketball!"
"Yes!" says Moon Man.
"Basketball is fun on the moon!"

"I bet I can dunk on the moon, too!"
says Dunk. "This is cool."
"Yes, it is," says Slam.
"But we need to go back."

They all go back.

Down, down, down zips the ship.

"Thanks!" say Slam and Dunk.
"Thank you!" Moon Man says.

"Mom, we had a ball game
on the moon with Moon Man,"
says Slam.

"What fun!" Slam's mom says.